WITHDRAWN

P9-DUM-414

# The Symphony That Was Silent

by
Steve Brezenoff

illustrated by
Marcos Calo

STONE ARCH BOOKS
a capstone imprint

r Samantha Archer,

Field Trip Mysteries are published by Stone Arch Books
A Capstone Imprint
1710 Roe Crest Drive
North Mankato, Minnesota 56003
www.capstonepub.com

Copyright © 2012 by Stone Arch Books
All rights reserved. No part of this publication may be
reproduced in whole or in part, or stored in a retrieval
system, or transmitted in any form or by any means,
electronic, mechanical, photocopying, recording,
or otherwise, without written permission of the publisher.

Library of Congress Cataloging-in-Publication Data

Brezenoff, Steven.
   The symphony that was silent / by Steve Brezenoff ;
illustrated by Marcos Calo.
      p. cm. --  (Field trip mysteries)
   ISBN-13: 978-1-4342-3226-7 (library binding)
   ISBN-13: 978-1-4342-3429-2 (pbk.)
   1.  Flute--Juvenile fiction. 2.  Orchestra--Juvenile
fiction. 3.  Theft--Juvenile fiction. 4.  School field
trips--Juvenile fiction. 5.  Detective and mystery
stories. [1. Mystery and detective stories. 2. School
field trips--Fiction. 3. Orchestra--Fiction.]  I. Calo,
Marcos, ill. II. Title. III. Series: Brezenoff, Steven.
Field trip mysteries.
   PZ7.B7576Sy 2011
   813.6--dc22

                                     2011002171

Art Director/Graphic Designer:
Kay Fraser

Summary: On a class trip to the symphony,
James "Gum" Shoo and his friends solve
the mystery of the stolen flute.

Printed in the United States of America in Stevens Point,
Wisconsin.
082013              007679R

# TABLE OF CONTENTS

Chapter One
**CONCERT BOUND** ........7

Chapter Two
**FANCY PANTS** ..............16

Chapter Three
**THE FLUTE** ..................26

Chapter Four
**STOLEN!** ......................34

Chapter Five
**SNEAK PEEK** ...............44

Chapter Six
**RUNNING OUT OF TIME** ...52

Chapter Seven
**ANTON** .....................................60

Chapter Eight
**OPPORTUNITY** ....................64

Chapter Nine
**NICE CANE** ...........................71

STUDENTS

**James Shoo**

A.K.A: (Gum)

D.O.B: November 19th

POSITION: 6th Grade

*Is this because he chews a lot of gum?*

**INTERESTS:**

Gum-chewing, field trips, and showing everyone what a crook Anton Gutman is.

**KNOWN ASSOCIATES:**

Archer, Samantha; Duran, Catalina; and Garrison, Edward.

**NOTES:**

Mr. Spade has made an effort to sto James from chewing gum in class. W fear he cannot be stopped.

CHAPTER ONE

**CONCERT BOUND**

Anton Gutman and
I hardly ever agree.
In fact, he's probably my least
favorite person in the whole world.

I think he's a bully, and I'm sure he's a huge crook, too. I haven't been able to prove it yet, but someday I'll catch him in the act.

We do agree about two things, though. I know this because I overheard him on the bus on the way to Symphony Hall for our latest field trip.

My friends and I were way in the back of the bus. We were all dressed up in our best clothes. Anton was a couple of rows ahead of us.

"I can't believe we're going to listen to some stupid orchestra," Anton said. He groaned and made a face, pulling at his collar. "And the collar of this shirt is making me crazy!"

"Never thought I'd agree with Anton," I whispered to Egg, one of my best friends.

"What do you mean?" Egg whispered back.

I groaned and said, "This tie is so annoying."

All the boys were in suits, or nice pants and nice jackets. All the girls were in dresses.

Well, almost all the girls.

Not Sam — her name is short for Samantha, and she's one of my best friends too. She was wearing a man's suit. It looked like it was probably her grandfather's. She lives with her grandparents, and she's always raiding their closets.

Sam sat in the seat across the aisle from me. Next to her at the window seat was Catalina, another of my best friends, who we always just call Cat. Cat was in a pink dress, and her hair was done up nicely.

"You look nice in your dress," I told her.

"Dresses are too girly for me," Sam said, smiling. She tipped her hat at me and I laughed.

Egg sat next to me. "I'm used to you talking like your grandfather by now, Sam," he said. "But dressing like him too? That's a new one."

"Hey, if you boys don't have to wear a dress, I don't see why I should have to!" Sam said loudly.

A voice shouted from the front of the bus: "Keep it down back there!"

It was Mr. Forte, our music teacher. He was in the front of the bus with his big headphones on.

"I can hear your screaming over my Beethoven," he said. "Quiet down, kids."

Beethoven was Mr. Forte's favorite composer. This field trip was to see an orchestra play some of Beethoven's music at Symphony Hall. It was a very big deal, which is why we had to get all dressed up.

Mr. Forte was in a tuxedo, but he still didn't look dressed up. He looked like he'd slept in the tuxedo, rolled out of bed, and gotten on the bus with us.

"Sorry, Mr. Forte," Cat called out with a smile. "We'll be quieter."

"All right," Mr. Forte said. "Thanks."

He smiled back at her. All the teachers love Cat.

Then Mr. Forte went back to enjoying the music in his headphones. He bopped his head and waved his arms around like a crazy person.

Egg pulled out his camera and took a few pictures. "Look at these, Gum," he said.

That's me. I'm James Shoo, but everyone calls me Gum.

I took the camera and flipped through the pictures on the display. They were great shots of Mr. Forte, conducting the invisible orchestra in the front seat.

"Good pictures," I said. "You really captured the motion of his **crazy arms.**"

"Thanks," Egg said. His name is really Edward, but everyone calls him Egg. "It should be fun to watch Mr. Forte listening to live Beethoven music. He'll probably jump up and start conducting from the audience."

The bus parked in front of Symphony Hall. The brakes squeaked, and the door creaked. Mr. Forte finally took off his headphones and stood up.

"Here we are, everyone," he said. His smile was humongous. "Get ready for the premiere of 'The Third Symphony'!" Then he clapped, like he thought everyone else would start clapping too.

When no one did, he led us off the bus.

"The premiere of what?" I whispered to Cat as we headed up the aisle toward the door.

"'The Third Symphony,'" she said. "That's the name of the symphony we're seeing today. Don't you ever pay attention in class?"

I shrugged. "If I can get through this without falling asleep," I said, "it'll be a miracle."

Anton overheard me. "I'm with you, dork," he said. "This will be one boring afternoon."

We followed Mr. Forte into Symphony Hall. The place was packed! Once we passed the ticket windows, where most people had to stop to have their tickets checked, we entered a huge entryway.

The ceilings were very high, and covered in paintings and gold leaf. In front of us was a pair of big curved staircases.

A sign near the stairs had an arrow pointing up. It read, "To the balcony."

"Wow," Cat said. "This place is so fancy."

Sam nodded. "I feel like I'm in an old crime movie or something," she said. "This would be the perfect first scene. It's so cool and old-fashioned."

Anton and his two goon friends pushed past us. "Since when did 'cool' and 'old-fashioned' ever describe the same thing?" Anton asked, rolling his eyes. "This place is the opposite of cool."

Luckily, I didn't agree with Anton. I thought that Symphony Hall was very cool, even if it was old-fashioned. But as usual, I was glad to see Anton and his friends disappearing into the crowd. That guy can be a real creep.

Egg thought Symphony Hall was really cool too. He snapped lots of pictures, until a man in a tuxedo tapped him on the shoulder.

# "Turn off your flash,"
## the man said.

He pointed to a sign on the wall that said "No flash photography." This guy's tux wasn't all wrinkled like Mr. Forte's was.

"Oh, sorry," Egg said. He clicked a button on his camera. "I didn't see the sign."

The man nodded. Then he looked at Sam. "Young man," he said, "please remove your hat. It is rude to wear a hat indoors."

Sam squinted at the man. "Me?" she asked.

"Is there another young man in a hat standing here?" the man asked, sticking his nose in the air. I thought he was very rude.

Sam shrugged and pulled off her hat. Then she shook her head so her long blond hair fell over her shoulders. The man's jaw dropped.

"Is that better?" Sam asked. Cat covered her mouth so she wouldn't giggle.

The man just nodded, his mouth still open, and walked away.

Egg elbowed me in the ribs. "Look at that guy," he said, pointing toward the door.

A tall, bearded, and obviously very rich man was coming in. He was dressed better than anyone else in the place, maybe better than anyone else I'd ever seen.

I noticed he walked with a slight limp. In his right hand, he had a cane.

Even the cane was fancy. It had a gold ball on top, and it looked like a diamond was set right into the gold.

He had three big men with him, walking very close to him and wearing sunglasses. They were obviously his bodyguards.

Egg took a few pictures. Of course.

The man and his bodyguards were following another man. He was smiling nervously and walking stooped over. He was in a tuxedo too, but it didn't look very fancy, like the other guy's did. This guy's tux made him look like a waiter.

"Right this way, Mr. Glissando," the man said. "We can begin your VIP tour."

Mr. Glissando, the fancy guy, nodded. The group went through a door behind the staircases.

Sam whistled. "Get a load of him," she said. "Think he's royalty?"

A moment later, we saw another man walking through the room. He was in a long, tan coat and a hat like Sam's, and he had a big bushy mustache. He was actually very funny-looking.

The man lingered by the door behind the staircase. Egg, with his flash still off, snapped a photo.

"Hey," Sam said. "Why didn't anyone tell him to take off his hat?"

The man looked around the room. Then he opened the door behind the stairs and followed the first group.

"Well, he's up to something, isn't he?" Gum said. "Maybe this trip won't be so boring after all."

Cat wasn't paying attention to the man with the mustache and the big trench coat. She was looking at something else. I tried to see what she was staring at.

"What's happening?" I asked.

Cat pointed at a crowd gathering between the staircases. "I'm not sure," she said. "But something's going on."

"Let's join them," Sam said.

So we did.

We managed to squeeze to the front of the big crowd of people. Mr. Forte was right there, looking very excited. He practically jumped up and down when he saw us. "Can you believe it?" he said.

"Um . . . believe what?" Sam asked.

We looked around to see what everyone was waiting for. We were all gathered around an empty glass case.

"This is weird," I said. "Why is everyone so excited about an empty case?"

"The flute will be brought out at any moment," Mr. Forte said.

"What flute?" I asked.

"A very old and famous flute," Mr. Forte said. "It's been touring the world. A very similar one was stolen in Europe recently."

"Stolen?
By who?"
Sam asked.

"A famous thief of musical instruments," Mr. Forte said. We all gathered closer to listen to him. "His name is Baron Hans van Beckert," Mr. Forte went on. "But no one has ever even seen him. He's always in disguise and escapes easily."

"Wow," Cat said.

"Why is the flute here?" Sam asked.

"To celebrate the premiere of 'The Third Symphony' tonight," Mr. Forte said. "The anonymous owner of the flute offered it. You see, 'The Third Symphony' has a beautiful flute part. It was really a very nice thing to do. I'm sure the orchestra's flautist is very excited. Perhaps almost as excited as I am!"

My friends and I glanced at each other.

Mr. Forte's face lit up as he watched the door. "Ah, here it comes now," he said.

The door behind the staircases opened, and two men in uniforms came out. With them was the man who'd led Mr. Glissando into the back.

The man was smiling and looked very proud, and he was carrying a small leather case. He held up the case and everyone in the crowd said, "Oooh."

"Ladies and gentlemen," the man said. "I am Geoffrey Jaffrey, the manager of Symphony Hall. It is my great pleasure to reveal the special guest for tonight's performance of Beethoven's 'Third Symphony'."

He put the case down on the glass. "Here is the famous flute," he said.

Everyone leaned forward. The whole crowd seemed to be holding their breath.

"I'd like to remind you," Mr. Jaffrey went on, "this is a solid gold flute. It was made by Theobald Boehm. He was the greatest designer of flutes ever. It is priceless."

He ran a hand over the leather case and smiled at the crowd. Someone at the back shouted, "Open it already, Jaffrey!"

Mr. Jaffrey cleared his throat. "And now, the flute!" he said. And he opened the case.

Everyone gasped.

Mr. Forte let out a little scream.

The case was empty.

The whole crowd went silent. Mr. Jaffrey still hadn't noticed that the case was empty, but of course everyone gathered around us had.

Mr. Jaffrey just stood there, smiling. I think he started to wonder why no one was clapping or jumping up and down. I looked over at Mr. Forte, who looked like he might pass out.

Finally someone said in a quiet voice, "It's . . . it's gone."

The manager's eyes went wide and he turned the case around. "Gone?" he said.

"The flute was stolen!" someone cried from the crowd.

Sam grabbed my elbow and pulled me out of the crowd. Egg and Cat followed.

"We're on the case," Sam said.

We all nodded. Egg patted his camera. "I've been snapping pictures since we got here," he said. "I'll look through them. I'll see if I spot anything unusual in any of the photographs."

Sam tapped her nose. "Good thinking," she said.

Just then, we heard a bell ringing near the stairs.

"What's that? A bell?" Cat asked.

The manager was standing on the steps and hitting a triangle. Cat blushed when she saw him. "Well, it sounded like a bell at first," she said quietly.

Once the room got quiet enough, Mr. Jaffrey announced, "Ladies and gentlemen, I'm sorry to say that today's symphony performance will be canceled."

Everyone gasped.

"Unless we recover that priceless flute, we shall have to not only cancel tonight's show," Mr. Jaffrey went on, "but the rest of the season."

People started getting very upset. Mr. Glissando, that rich man, took a fan from his pocket and waved it in front of his face. He looked like he might pass out. His guards led him to a nearby bench to sit down.

The man in the long tan coat skulked around near the steps, looking at everyone. I tried to get a good look at his face, but I couldn't, because the brim of his hat was in the way.

Just then, a woman in a fancy dress came barging out of the back room. In one hand, she was holding a skinny stick. She strode up to the manager.

"Mr. Jaffrey!" she yelled.

"That must be the conductor," Cat whispered. "That thing is called a baton."

"Ah, Ms. Pianissimo," the manager said. He seemed very nervous. "I can see that you're upset."

"Of course I am upset!" the conductor said. "It was very difficult to get that flute. You promised that it would be safe here."

She pointed her baton at Mr. Jaffrey.

"This is not the first time I've been disappointed by this place," Ms. Pianissimo said. "There was the problem with the heat this summer."

"Right," Mr. Jaffrey said.

"Then the air conditioner wouldn't shut off all winter!" Ms. Pianissimo yelled.

"I know," Mr. Jaffrey said.

"I've been looking for a reason to leave, and this security problem is the last straw!" Ms. Pianissimo shouted. "If you do not improve this hall and get that flute back, I shall leave at once. And I'll take my orchestra with me."

"But, Ms. Pianissimo," Mr. Jaffrey said, "where else will you play?"

"Anywhere
but here!"
the conductor said.

"I hear there's an empty warehouse near the river," Ms. Pianissimo went on. "You signed a contract. That means you'll have to pay me and my orchestra for the next three years. Even if we're not playing here. How will you like that?"

Mr. Jaffrey began to laugh, but Ms. Pianissimo did not even smile. She clearly wasn't joking at all.

"Oh," Mr. Jaffrey said. His smile fell away. "I promise you, we will find that flute."

The conductor shook her head. Then she stormed toward the back again.

"Wow, she's really angry," Egg said.

He showed us a photo of Ms. Pianissimo's face. It was bright red with anger.

"I guess the conductor and the manager don't get along," Cat said.

"And maybe they never have," Sam said.

"Did we just find our first suspect?" I asked.

Sam shook her head. "We found a suspect," she said, "but not our first."

"There's Glissando again," I said. The man with the cane and his bodyguards were storming through the lobby.

"What kind of symphony hall is this?" Mr. Glissando was shouting.

The manager ran over to him.

"There you are, Mr. Jaffrey," Mr. Glissando said. His face kept getting redder and redder. "Is this catastrophe your fault?"

"I'm sure the flute will be found, sir," Mr. Jaffrey said quietly.

Mr. Glissando waved the manager off and shook his head. "I can't believe I planned to donate millions of dollars to this hall," Mr. Glissando said. "I won't give a dime to a place like this. A priceless flute, gone! Mr. Jaffrey, you'll be famous indeed — famous for losing this flute!"

Mr. Glissando pointed to a nearby bench. His guards led him over to it and helped him to sit down. "I get so tired when I'm angry," Mr. Glissando mumbled.

"Ah, there you four are," Mr. Forte said, walking up to us. "The rest of the class is already waiting for our tour."

"Tour?" I asked. "We're having a tour?"

Mr. Forte nodded. "Because the symphony will not be happening," he said, "I asked Mr. Jaffrey to give us a short tour of the hall."

"Oh, what a thrill," I said quietly.

"Shh," Sam said. "This will be a great chance to look for clues."

Mr. Forte led us to the door behind the stairs. The rest of the class was already there. They were waiting for us and Mr. Jaffrey.

A moment later, Mr. Jaffrey walked up. The manager pulled out his keys and opened the door.

"I'll be with you in a moment," he said. "Don't touch anything!"

Mr. Forte went in first. My friends and I were right behind him. Just as we stepped into the room, Mr. Forte flicked on the lights. A figure darted across the room and out a side door.

"What was that?" I asked.

"I saw a tan coat," Cat said. "I think."

"I bet it was that weird skulking guy," Egg said. He showed us a photo he had taken. The guy was wearing a long tan coat.

The back room was not as cool as the lobby. It was just a big room with shelves and cubbies along the walls. The walls were painted black.

Mr. Jaffrey came in then. "This is where the flute was being stored," he said. "Obviously the crook took it from this room."

Mr. Forte was standing near the cases along the wall.

"This way, please," Mr. Jaffrey said. "I'll show you the main hall and the stage."

The class gathered near the manager, but Mr. Forte didn't move a single inch. He was just staring at the instruments stored in the cubbies.

"Can I help you, Mr. Forte?" Mr. Jaffrey said.

Mr. Forte jumped. "Oh, excuse me," he said. "I was just looking at these instruments. I collect old instruments, you know. Some of these are very lovely."

"Is that right?" Mr. Jaffrey asked.

I looked at Sam. I knew she was thinking what I was thinking.

Was Mr. Forte on our suspect list now?

Mr. Forte pointed at a violin. "This is a beauty, isn't it?" he said. "Not as beautiful as the missing flute, of course. But very nice."

"Indeed," Mr. Jaffrey said. He walked over to Mr. Forte.

Our teacher strolled over to a curved brass instrument. "This French horn is also a very good example," he said.

He ran a finger along the bell of the
French horn.

Mr. Jaffrey slapped Mr. Forte's hand away.
"Please do not touch," he said. Then he took
Mr. Forte by the arm. "Now, let's move on
with the tour."

"Yes, of course," Mr. Forte said. But I could
tell he didn't want to leave those instruments.

After the tour, most of the people had left the hall. Our class was hanging around in the lobby. "It's already 5:30," Cat said, showing us her watch.

"If they don't find that flute in the next thirty minutes, I guess there's no concert," Egg said.

"Oh, no!" Cat said. "What a horrible field trip this is turning out to be!"

"That's okay with me," I said. "In fact, I hope they don't find it."

"What?" Sam said. "Then a crook will get away with that flute!"

I shrugged. "Okay, so I don't want anyone to get away with stealing," I said, "but I sure don't mind missing a boring old concert."

"Oh really?" Sam asked. She sneered and got right in my face. "Perhaps we can add one more to our suspect list!"

"Me?" I asked, backing up. "That's ridiculous."

"Is it?" Sam said, narrowing her eyes. "That remains to be seen. Let's go over who we have so far."

"The skulking guy in the long coat," Egg said. "He sure acts suspiciously."

"Really? Hmm. I don't think it's him," Sam said.

"You don't?"
I asked. "He's my
top choice as
the culprit."

Sam winked at me. "Call it a hunch," she said.

"There's also the conductor," Cat said. "She was just so angry, and obviously hates Symphony Hall."

"And Anton Gutman," I said. "Always Anton Gutman."

"Right," Sam said. She glared at me. "Why Anton?"

"Well, you heard him," I said. "He'd like nothing more than to miss this concert."

"Reminds me of someone else who also wants to miss the concert," Cat said. "Hey, Egg and Sam, doesn't the way Anton is acting remind you guys of someone? Someone else who's been whining about the concert all day?"

They both nodded.

"Okay, fine," I said, throwing my hands up. "So count me as a suspect. But we can rule me out pretty quickly too. I definitely have an alibi."

"What's your alibi?" Sam asked.

"I was with you three, obviously," I said. I rolled my eyes.

"Oh, good point," Sam said. "Okay, you're off the hook."

"Thank you," I said. "But we have one more suspect. Mr. Forte."

"Our teacher?" Cat asked. "Oh, it couldn't have been him."

"Why not?" Sam asked. "He loves instruments. You saw him drool all over that trumpet."

"French horn," Egg said.

"Whatever," Sam said. "I think he's definitely a suspect, and a strong one, too."

"I can't believe it," Egg said. "He loves music too much to do anything like this."

"Hmm," I said. "Maybe. Or maybe he loves music too much to resist doing something like this!"

Cat sighed. She pointed to a vacant bench and we headed over to sit down.

I sat down on the bench and groaned. "Guys, we have a long list of suspects," I said. "We have to start narrowing it down."

"Where do we start?" Egg asked.

Sam looked at her notebook, where she'd written down the names of our suspects.

Cat nibbled her fingernail.

"Don't think too hard," I said.

Then I pointed at three other students in the corner. They were laughing and hiding something.

"There's our prime suspect," I said. "Anton Gutman."

We headed toward Anton and his friends. When they saw us coming, they darted for the door and went outside. We followed them.

Anton and the goons started running, but so did we. Sam has really long legs, so she caught up to them in no time. Then she waited for the rest of us.

"What are you crooks up to?" Sam asked when we caught up.

They laughed.

"None of your business, nerds," Anton said. "Go away."

I went over to Anton and put an arm around his shoulder. He shook me off. "What do you know, Anton?" I said. "I guess we won't have to sit through some dumb symphony after all."

"Guess not," he said. He held up his watch. "They have like fifteen minutes to find that dumb flute. Then we can go home."

"Did you take it?" Sam snapped. She got right in Anton's face.

Anton pushed her away. "Relax, Archer," he said. "I didn't take the precious flute. But if I meet the one who did, I'll shake their hand." Then he and his henchmen went back inside.

We went back to our bench and sat down.

"This isn't getting us anywhere," I said, looking at my friends. "How can we prove Anton did it?"

"I really don't think he did," Egg said. He pulled out his camera and showed us some pictures. "See?" Egg said. "Anton and his friends are in almost every single one of my shots, in the background. There's no way he would've had time to go into the room without us noticing."

"So who had time?" Sam asked. She looked at her list of suspects and crossed off my name and Anton's name. "The conductor must have."

"And she had a motive," Cat said. "She was really mad about a lot of stuff. It sounded to me like she wouldn't mind seeing this hall shut down."

"She couldn't be serious about having her orchestra play in a warehouse, though," Egg said.

"It's possible," Cat said, frowning. She was obviously hurt that Egg hadn't taken her idea seriously.

"Who else could have done it?" Sam asked.

"Not Mr. Forte," Cat said. "He was with us."

"He's missing from a lot of my photos," Egg said. "Maybe he snuck into the back room and —"

Cat snapped her fingers. "The back room!" she said. "That's it! We saw a few people go back there right before the flute turned up missing."

"Exactly. Like Mr. Glissando!" Sam said.

"Sure, and the tan coat skulking guy, right behind him," Egg said. "See?" He showed us a photo of the man in the tan coat going through the door behind the stairs.

"Okay, so they both had the opportunity," I said. "That means it must be the weird guy in the coat."

Sam smiled at me. It was one of her crafty smiles. "What makes you say that?" she asked.

"Well, a rich guy like Glissando," I said. "What motive could he have?"

"Yeah," Cat said. "He's a millionaire, maybe a billionaire. He was even going to give the hall a bunch of money. Why would he steal the flute?"

"That's true," Sam said. "But . . . Egg, do you have a photo of Glissando going into the back room?"

Egg clicked through his pictures until he found one. "Here," he said. "It's not very interesting."

Just then, Glissando and his guards came out of the men's room.

Glissando adjusted his glasses and rubbed his beard. Then he started walking across the room toward Mr. Jaffrey, tapping his cane on the ground with his left hand.

The manager looked very worried and upset.

"Your time is up," Mr. Glissando said. "This will mean the end of Symphony Hall."

"And good riddance," Ms. Pianissimo said. "My orchestra and I will play somewhere else."

Glissando snapped his fingers and headed for the door.

"Egg," I said. "Show me that picture again."

I looked at the photo, then back at Mr. Glissando as he walked away. Then I looked at the picture again.

"Hey, Sam," I said. "Do you see what I see?"

She nodded slowly. "I do," she said.

"Do you have evidence against Mr. Glissando?" Cat asked. "I thought we were sure it wasn't him, since he's so rich already."

"We better find the guy in the coat," Sam said. "And quick."

"What?" Egg said. "Did you find evidence against Glissando or the weird guy? Let us in on it, will you!"

"No time," I said. I took Cat's elbow. "There he is. Let's hurry."

The man in the long, tan coat was kneeling in the corner behind a group of musicians. Their instruments were leaning against the wall next to him, but none of the musicians seemed to notice he was even there.

The man in the coat had a viola case opened, and he was examining the instrument very closely.

Sam tiptoed up behind him and put a finger in his back.

"Turn around," she said in a funny voice, like one of those men in the movies she likes. "Slowly."

He put up his hands and stood up. "Don't shoot," he said. "I'm a cop!"

Then he saw who had threatened him. He smirked at Sam. "You kids," he said. "I hope you're not here investigating."

It was Detective Jones, our old pal from the police force. He'd helped us on more than one crime-solving field trip.

"Detective!" Cat said, smiling.

"Oh, it's you!" Egg said, laughing. "Detective Jones, how are you?"

Sam had realized it was Detective Jones first. Then I'd figured it out too, when Sam was hinting that the guy in the tan coat couldn't have been the crook.

"Not good," the detective said. "I have about ten seconds to solve this crime or the symphony is doomed."

"Well, then, your troubles are over," I said. "It was Glissando. Right, Sam?"

"Not exactly," Sam said. "It was the man with the cane, but his name isn't Glissando. It's Baron Hans von Beckert."

"The baron?" Detective Jones repeated. "He's here?"

"In the flesh," Sam said. "The glasses, beard, and the cane are fakes. The cane is how we figured it out."

"Oh, and when he was in the men's room," Egg said, "he was fixing his disguise. That's why he was playing with his beard when he came out."

"And it's why his cane kept switching hands," I added. "And why his limp changed from one leg to the other."

Cat nodded. "Good job, Gum," she said.

Detective Jones nodded. "It must be the baron," he said. Then he pulled off his coat. Underneath, he was in a simple suit almost exactly like Sam's. They looked pretty funny standing next to each other.

Glissando and his guards were almost to the exit door.

Detective Jones ran across the room and blocked the exit — just as Glissando and his guards reached it.

"Not so fast," the detective said. He took out his badge. "You're under arrest, Baron."

"Baron?" the rich man repeated. "You must be mistaken. My name is Bennito Glissando."

"Is that right?" the detective asked.

Quick as lightning, he grabbed the rich man's beard and tugged it right off.

Mr. Jaffrey came running over. "What is going on here?" he asked.

"This isn't Bennito Glissando," Detective Jones told him. "This is Baron Hans von Beckert."

"How did you know?" the baron asked.

"These kids," the detective said. "I suspected the baron would show up here, but when there was no sign of him, I was stumped. Thankfully, these kids spotted your disguise."

The baron glared at us. We smiled back at him. "Fine, so you've shown my true identity," the baron said. "You have no evidence. I didn't steal that flute."

"I believe you did," the detective said. With his super quick hands, he grabbed the rich man's cane.

"Hey!" the baron said. "Give that back. I need it to walk."

We laughed. Detective Jones didn't give the cane back. He shook it. Then he put his ear to it. Finally, he pressed his thumb on the diamond set in the gold ball at the top.

The bottom of the cane popped open. Detective Jones slid two flutes into his hand. "You're under arrest, Baron Hans von Beckert," Detective Jones said. "And Mr. Jaffrey, here's your golden flute." He checked his watch and added, "Just in time."

The manager took it and held it up. "The show will go on!" he shouted. "The symphony is saved." Mr. Forte ran into the room, squealing with glee.

From across the room, we heard Anton and his henchmen groan. I could hardly blame them.

## literary news

# MYSTERIOUS WRITER REVEALED!

Steve Brezenoff lives in St. Paul, Minnesota, with his wife, Beth, their son, Sam, and their small, smelly dog, Harry. Besides writing books, he enjoys playing video games, riding his bicycle, and helping middle-school students work on their writing skills. Steve's ideas almost always come to him in his dreams, so he does his best writing in his pajamas.

## arts & entertainment

# CALIFORNIA ARTIST IS KEY TO SOLVING MYSTERY – POLICE SAY

Marcos Calo lives happily in A Coruña, Spain, with his wife, Patricia (who is also an illustrator), and their daughter, Claudia. When Marcos and Patricia aren't drawing, they like to go on long walks by the sea. They also watch a lot of films and eat Nutella sandwiches. Yum!

# A Detective's Dictionary

**alibi** (AL-i-bye)—a claim that a person accused of a crime was somewhere else when the crime was committed

**anonymous** (uh-NON-uh-muhss)—a person whose name is not known or made public

**baron** (BA-ruhn)—a nobleman

**baton** (buh-TON)—a thin stick used by a conductor to beat time for an orchestra

**conductor** (kuhn-DUHK-tur)—someone who stands in front of a group of musicians and directs it as it plays

**direct** (duh-REKT)—lead an orchestra or group of musicians

**evidence** (EV-uh-duhnss)—information and facts that help prove something

**flautist** (FLAU-tist)—a person who plays the flute

**premiere** (pre-MIHR)—the first public performance of a work of music

**skulking** (SKUHLK-ing)—being creepy or sneaky

**suspect** (SUH-spekt)—a person who may have committed a crime

Rare Musical Instruments

Some musical instruments are among the world's most expensive and rarest items. People love to own these instruments. Usually, they are treated as works of art, not played, but sometimes music enthusiasts do use their expensive musical instruments to play and compose music.

Sometimes musical instruments are considered more valuable because of previous owners. For example, the piano owned by one of the Beatles, John Lennon, sold for about two million dollars in 2000. It was purchased by the musician George Michael. Singer-songwriter Eric Clapton's guitar sold for almost a million dollars in 2004. Jazz great Dizzi Gillespie's trumpet was purchased in 1995 for #55,000. And part of The Who drummer Keith Mo drum set sold for over #200,000.

Previous owners aren't the only reason some instruments are valuable. Often it's the creator or design that makes it valuable. In 2005, a Stradivarius violin made in 1699 sold for more than two million dollars. Other Stradivarius violins, violas, and cellos from the seventeenth and eighteenth centuries have sold for more than one million dollars each. A Couchet harpsichord built in 1679 sold in 2001 for more than #300,000. And the world's most expensive flute, a platinum Powell flute, was purchased in 1986 for #186,000.

James: What a fabulous essay! Oh, how I would love to see those instruments. Do you think George Michael would let me come over and play John Lennon's piano? I wish I had enough money to buy one of these wonderful things! Thank you!

-Mr. Forte

# FURTHER INVESTIGATIONS

CASE #FTM12GSH

1. In this book, my class went on a field trip. What field trips have you gone on? Which one was your favorite, and why?

2. Why did the baron steal the flute?

3. Who else could have been a suspect in this mystery?

# IN YOUR OWN DETECTIVE'S NOTEBOOK . . .

1. What kind of music is your favorite? Write about it.

2. Gum, Egg, Cat, and I are best friends. Write about your best friend. Don't forget to include what you like about your friend.

3. This book is a mystery story. Write your own mystery story!

# THEY SOLVE CRIMES, CATCH CROOKS, CRACK CODES,

## ...AND RIDE THE BUS BACK TO SCHOOL AFTERWARD.

Meet Egg, Gum, Sam, and Cat.
Four sixth-grade detectives and best
friends. Wherever field trips take them,
mysteries aren't far behind!

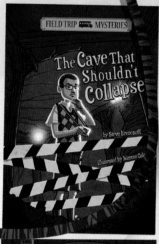

FIELD TRIP MYSTERIES

The Cave That Shouldn't Collapse

by Steve Brezenoff

Illustrated by Marcos Calo

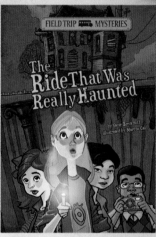

FIELD TRIP MYSTERIES

The Ride That Was Really Haunted

by Steve Brezenoff

Illustrated by Marcos Calo

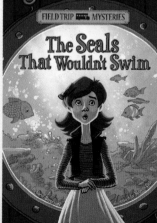

FIELD TRIP MYSTERIES

The Seals That Wouldn't Swim

by Steve Brezenoff

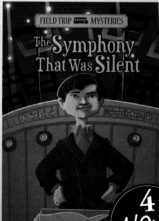

FIELD TRIP MYSTERIES

The Symphony That Was Silent

by Steve Brezenoff

Illustrated by Marcos Calo

4 New Mysteries

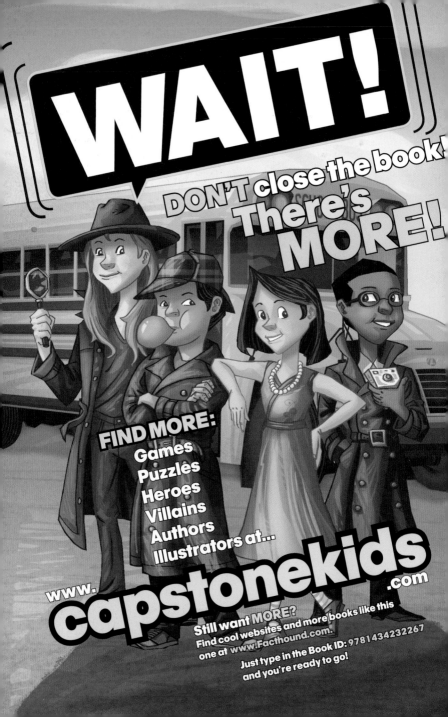

# WAIT!

## DON'T close the book! There's MORE!

**FIND MORE:**
Games
Puzzles
Heroes
Villains
Authors
Illustrators at...

www. **capstonekids** .com

**Still want MORE?**
Find cool websites and more books like this
one at www.Facthound.com.

Just type in the Book ID: 9781434232267
and you're ready to go!

31901059455511